Moon Glowing

by **Elizabeth Partridge**

illustrated by **Joan Paley**

Dutton Children's Books • New York

Autumn leaves twirling down.

Squirrel leaping,

bat swooping,

beaver gnawing.

Bear, big bear, feasting well.

Icy winds blowing through.

Squirrel stashing,

bat chewing,

beaver building.

Bear, big bear, digging deep.

Winter clouds rolling in.

Squirrel peeking,

bat scrambling,

beaver listening.

Bear, big bear, squeezing in.

Soft new snow falling down.

Nose tucking,

wings folding,

eyes closing.

Paws, big paws, wrapping round.

Deep white snow covering all.

Clouds parting,

stars shining,

wind whispering.

Moon, big moon, glowing bright.

All sleeping, sleeping tight.

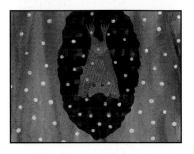

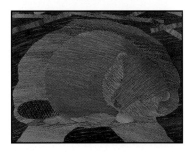

When cold autumn winds blow, animals get ready for winter.

TREE SQUIRRELS bury nuts in the ground and make warm nests in hollow trees. During winter, they come out during the day to search for food and to dig up the nuts they hid. Squirrels can smell their buried nuts under a foot of snow!

Getting ready for the cold weather, some BATS catch as many as 1,200 mosquitoes and other insects an hour — that's one insect every three seconds. While some kinds of bats migrate south for the winter, others hibernate. They scramble under loose bark or shingles, or hang upside down in an attic or cave. The bat's heartbeat and breathing slow way down during hibernation, and its body temperature drops to just above freezing.

BEAVERS work all year to dam up streams and build strong lodges from branches and caked mud. The only way in and out of their lodges is through a hole in the floor that leads right into the water. Beavers sleep most of the winter, waking up occasionally to chew the bark off branches they've piled in their lodges. They also plunge down into the water to go to the bathroom and to eat from branches they have stuck in the mud of the lake.

Before winter sets in, BEARS can gain up to forty pounds of fat per week. They gorge on berries, nuts, seeds, fish, eggs, and small animals. When the weather gets cold, they dig a den or find a cave to shelter in. The bear's body temperature drops a few degrees, and its heart rate and breathing slow down. Bears can wake up and go back to sleep during hibernation, but for months they don't eat or go to the bathroom. Some scientists now call them "super-hibernators."

In spring, the weather warms up and the snow melts. Bears and bats come out of hibernation to hunt for food, and squirrels and beavers find tender shoots and flowers to eat.

To my beautiful nephew Walter   —E.P.

To "Preserve Our Pond," which is leading the way in restoring and protecting lakes and ponds in our Commonwealth   —J.P.

Text copyright © 2002 by Elizabeth Partridge • Illustrations copyright © 2002 by Joan Paley
All rights reserved. • CIP Data is available.

Published in the United States 2002 by Dutton Children's Books,
a division of Penguin Young Readers Group
345 Hudson Street, New York, New York 10014 • www.penguinputnam.com

Designed by Ellen M. Lucaire and Gloria Cheng
Printed in China • First Edition • 10 9 8 7 6 5 4 3 2
ISBN 0-525-46873-0

The collage illustrations for this book were made with shapes cut from different papers. The shapes were painted with watercolors and textured with crayon, pastel, colored pencils, and oil paints.